The Enchanted STORKS

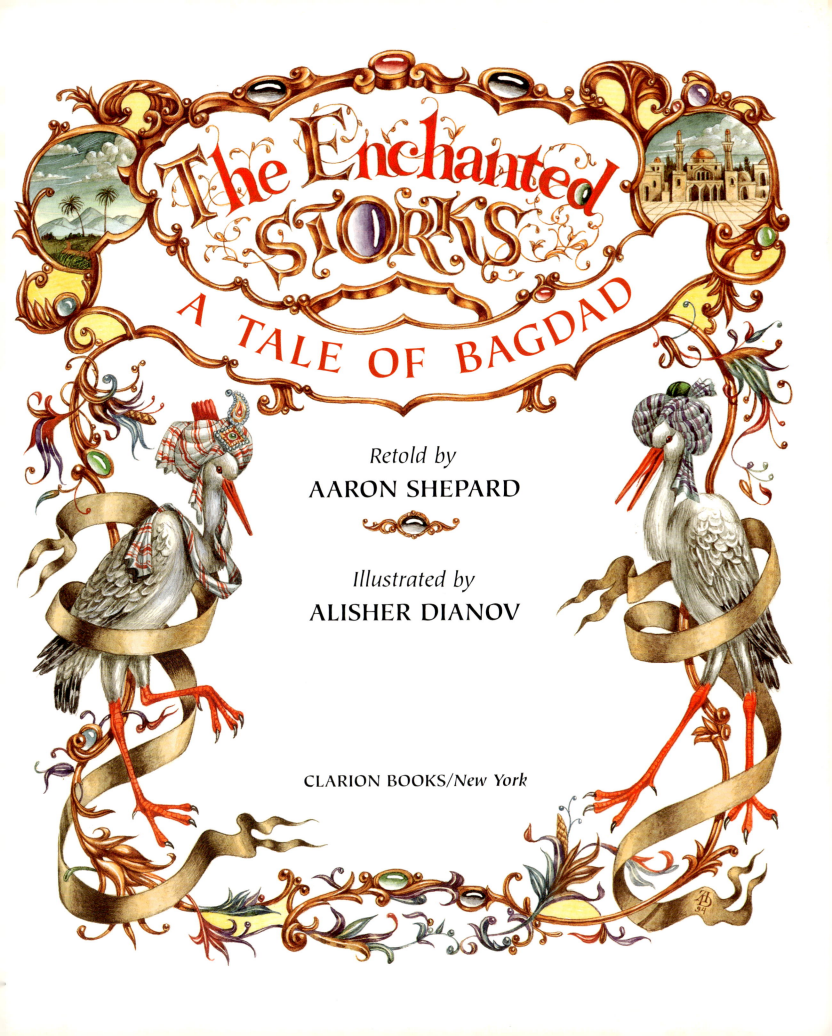

The Enchanted STORKS
A TALE OF BAGDAD

Retold by
AARON SHEPARD

Illustrated by
ALISHER DIANOV

CLARION BOOKS/New York

Clarion Books
a Houghton Mifflin Company imprint
215 Park Avenue South, New York, NY 10003
Text copyright © 1995 by Aaron Shepard
Illustrations copyright © 1995 by Alisher Dianov

The illustrations for this book were executed in watercolor
on cold-press paper.
The text was set in 16/20-point Garamond.

Printed in the USA

Library of Congress Cataloging-in-Publication Data

Shepard, Aaron.
The enchanted storks : a tale of Bagdad / retold by Aaron Shepard;
illustrated by Alisher Dianov.
p.   cm.
Retold from: Die Geschichte von Kaliph Storch / Wilhelm Hauff.
Summary: The Calif of Baghdad is turned into a stork by an evil sorcerer,
the only one who knows the magic word that will restore the Calif to his
human form.
ISBN 0-395-65377-0
[1. Fairy tales. 2. Folklore—Iraq.] I. Dianov, Alisher, ill.   II. Hauff,
Wilhelm, 1802–1827. Geschichte von Kaliph Storch.   III. Title.
PZ8.S3425En   1995
398.21—dc20   93-41540
[E]   CIP
                                                                 AC

HOR   10   9   8   7   6   5   4   3   2   1

For the people of Bagdad
—A.S.

For two wonderful women,
Nina and Irina,
with my deep appreciation
—A.D.

If favor now should greet my story,
Allah must receive the glory.

Once, in the great and glorious city of Bagdad, there was a Calif—Commander of the Faithful and ruler of all Islam. The people of Bagdad loved their ruler, yet one thing mystified them. All who came before him were amazed by his intimate knowledge of their daily lives.

"The Calif has a thousand eyes," muttered some, glancing behind them for spies. But the Calif's real secret was this: Each afternoon, he and his trusted Vizier, Ali ben Manzar, would disguise themselves as merchants and slip through a hidden door in the palace wall. Then they would roam the bazaars of the city, listening to the talk and gossip of the day.

One afternoon, as the Calif and his Vizier made their way through the market, an old and wizened man thrust one of his wares under the Calif's nose.

"What a lovely snuffbox!" said the Calif, admiring the carving and jeweled inlay. "What will you ask for it?"

"Just one gold coin," the peddler wheezed.

The Calif gave him two, took the box, and walked on.

Reaching the edge of the city, the Calif and his Vizier strolled through the parks and orchards beyond. At last they stopped to rest by a quiet lake.

"I wonder if my new box holds any snuff," said the Calif.

He opened the tiny box and found it filled with the pungent powder. "But what is this?" he said, pulling a piece of parchment from the underside of the lid.

The Vizier craned his neck to see. "What does it say, Glorious Lord?"

The Calif read,

> A sniff of snuff, for wings to soar.
> *Casalavair* for hands once more.

"Why, I believe the snuff is magic!" said the Calif. He looked longingly at the sky. "I have always wanted to see my city from the air."

"Perhaps we should be cautious," said the Vizier. "What if the charm fails to change us back?"

"If the snuff works, then surely the magic word will too," said the Calif. "Come, let us try our luck!"

He held out the box, and each took a pinch of snuff. Then together they inhaled the powder.

A flurry of wings, beaks, and feathers—and there in place of the Calif and his Vizier stood two storks.

"Wonderful!" the Calif said, snapping and clattering his beak—for that is how storks talk. A human would have heard only *Calap! Calap!* But since both the Calif and his Vizier were now birds, Ali ben Manzar understood perfectly.

Calap! Calap! "Quite amazing!" replied the Vizier.

Calap! Calap! "Let us test our wings!" said the Calif.

The two storks rose into the air, circling higher and higher. Spread below were meadows, ornamental gardens, orchards, and fields of crops. The great river Tigris flowed slowly across the plain, sprouting canals along its length. And basking on the banks of the river was Bagdad, capital of all Islam, City of Peace.

"Breathtaking, is it not?" called the Calif. "Come, let us fly over the city."

They soared above the streets, canals, bridges, and clay-brick buildings of Bagdad. In courtyard and bazaar, people bought and sold, worked and rested, fought and prayed, stole and chased, kissed and parted, laughed and wept.

"Truly," said the Calif, "a stork knows more of this city than the Calif himself."

As evening drew near, the Vizier called, "Glorious Lord, we had best return to the palace."

Back they flew to the lake, and landed by the snuffbox. The Calif once more read the parchment, then cried, "Casalavair!"

But nothing happened.

"Casalavair!" called the Calif again. "Casalavair! Casalavair!"

But storks they remained.

"Ali ben Manzar, you try it!" said the terrified Calif.

"Casalavair! Casalavair!" cried the no less terrified Vizier.

No matter how they called and hopped and flapped their wings, nothing changed.

"It seems," the Vizier said, "some enemy has lured us into this enchantment."

"What can we do?" asked the Calif.

"I know of nothing," said the Vizier. "Without the proper word to break the spell, we may never regain our true forms."

The sun dipped into the lake as the two storks stood lost in thought. Finally the Calif said, "Stork or not, my stomach aches for food. What are we to eat?"

"Why, Glorious Lord," said the Vizier, "we must eat what every stork eats! Fish and mice, frogs and toads, snakes and eels, snails and slugs, worms and grubs."

So the storks poked their beaks among rushes at the lake edge and into holes along the bank. When they had eaten as much as they could bear, each stood on one leg, crossed the other leg against it, hid his beak among his breast feathers, and slept.

The next morning, they hid the snuffbox and flew to the palace. From high on a turret they watched the frantic scene within the palace walls. Soldiers, courtiers, and servants rushed about in search of the Calif and the Vizier—a search the storks knew too well was in vain.

Suddenly, the Vizier cried out, "Look, Glorious Lord! A caravan approaches!"

Through the streets of Bagdad came a magnificent procession of horsemen, camel riders, and servants on foot. At its head rode a horseman in regal dress.

"By the beard of the Prophet," cried the Calif, "it is my brother Omar! He has long coveted my throne."

The caravan reached the gate, and the horseman called to the guards. "I am Omar, brother to the Calif. I have learned by secret means that the Calif is missing and will not return. As true successor of the Prophet Mohammed, I have come to take my brother's place as Commander of the Faithful, ruler of all Islam."

"Do not open the gate!" called the Calif.

But all that was heard by the startled people below was *Calap! Calap!* And when they looked up, all they saw was two storks—one of them hopping madly, flapping its wings and clattering its beak.

"You see?" exulted Omar. "Even the storks welcome me. Open the gate!"

The gate opened, and Omar rode through in triumph.

Up on the turret, the Calif stood silent and still.

"Glorious Lord," the Vizier said gently, "we can do nothing here. Let us fly far from the city. In solitude we may find the strength to bear our fate."

The two soared away, beyond the city and the plains, to a lonely forest in the foothills of the great mountains. There they began their new life. They dined on tree toads and fish, and tried not to speak of Bagdad or the affairs of a Calif.

One afternoon, the storks wandered into a different part of the forest. "How gloomy and silent it is here," said the Vizier. "Not even a rustle of leaves."

Just then, a quick *tap-tap-tap* made them jump. They turned to see a woodpecker hunting for worms in the bark of a tree. To their amazement, tears flowed from the woodpecker's eyes.

"Good woodpecker," said the Calif, "why do you weep?"

"Why should I not?" said the woodpecker. "You were born a bird and have known no other life, but I am a princess. The evil sorcerer Khadur threw this spell upon me, for I would not marry him. And a bird I must remain until another man asks me to wed. Imagine, a man proposing to a bird! Do you see now why I weep?"

"I do," the Calif said thoughtfully. "But how did you come to this forest? Is the sorcerer himself hereabouts?"

"There is a clearing nearby," she said. "He meets there every night with his magicians."

The Calif said to his Vizier, "Come, Ali ben Manzar. We may find a way to help our little friend—and perhaps ourselves as well."

The Calif and his Vizier followed the woodpecker through the thick forest until they reached a wide, rocky circle where no plant grew. They hid themselves in the bushes at its edge and waited for the gathering dark.

21

As the moon rose and cast its light into the clearing, three cloaked men entered the circle by different paths. They built a fire on a tall, flat rock in the very center and sat cross-legged around it. Then the flames leaped, and a fourth cloaked figure stood among them.

"Hail, Khadur, greatest of sorcerers!" the magicians shouted, touching their heads to the ground.

The Calif gasped. "By the beard of the Prophet! It is the peddler who sold us the box!"

Before the storks could recover from this surprise, there was another. With a clatter of hooves, into the clearing rode the Calif's brother, Omar.

"Greetings, sorcerer," said Omar as he pulled up before the fire.

"Greetings, Glorious Lord," the sorcerer wheezed. "And how do you fare in the city of Bagdad?"

"Excellently," said Omar. "The people long for their old ruler, but they learn to fear me and obey. As for you, sorcerer, you have well earned your reward." He threw Khadur a bulging pouch. "But you have not yet told me—how did you get rid of my brother?"

Khadur wheezed with laughter. "Nothing easier, Glorious Lord. I disguised myself as a peddler and sold him a box of magic snuff. Your brother and his dolt of a Vizier changed themselves most obligingly into storks! I even provided the word of disenchantment—or nearly so."

"What do you mean?" said Omar.

"I switched two letters," said Khadur. "I wrote *Casalavair* instead of *Calasavair*." The sorcerer laughed until he choked.

"A true master! I will have need of your services again," said Omar. He spurred his horse and raced from the clearing.

"Now, to work!" Khadur told his magicians. "We have spells to prepare."

"There will be no spells tonight!" cried the Calif.

All that the men heard was *Calap! Calap!*—but two storks were suddenly upon them, pummeling them with strong wings, pecking them with sharp beaks.

"It's the Calif and the Vizier!" wheezed Khadur. He fled from the clearing, his magicians close behind.

"Should we not follow, Glorious Lord?" asked the Vizier.

"No, Ali ben Manzar, we have spells to undo." Drawing an anxious breath, the Calif cried, "Calasavair!"

A flurry of wings, beaks, and feathers—and there in place of two storks stood the Calif and his Vizier.

Then, turning to the astonished woodpecker, the Calif said, "Princess, will you honor me by becoming my wife?"

Another flurry of feathers, and there stood a young woman of slender figure and dancing eyes.

"The honor will be mine," she said shyly, and offered him her hand.

The next day, they borrowed horses at a nearby village and rode into Bagdad. By the time they reached the palace, a joyous crowd had gathered behind them.

"Open the gate!" called the Calif.

The gate flew open just as Omar appeared in the palace yard. When Omar saw the Calif, he turned the color of parchment.

"Seize him!" the Calif ordered, and the guards dragged Omar before him.

"Brother, spare my life!" pleaded Omar.

"For your treason, I should behead you," said the Calif. "But instead I will banish you by ship to the farthest end of the earth. And by the beard of the Prophet, on the voyage you will eat nothing but toads and snails!"

And so the Calif regained his throne, and gained a lovely wife besides. And if he seemed to know even more about his people than before, no one guessed how—for few even noticed a pair of storks that soared on many an afternoon above the streets of Bagdad.

The Calif saw much more than we,
But how much more does Allah see!

About the Story

This tale—usually called "The Calif Stork" or "The Stork Calif"—is often classified as a folktale of Iraq, and folklorist Harold Courlander, who heard it twice from Muslim storytellers, believes it to be widely told in the Middle East. Yet its origin is *The Caravan,* a book of original fairy tales by nineteenth-century German writer Wilhelm Hauff. While folktales often make their way into written literature, in this case a written work has passed into folklore. My own retelling draws from both the original and retold versions.

The calif in this tale is patterned after Harun al-Rashid, made popular in the pages of *The Thousand and One Nights.* In Harun's time—around A.D. 800—the Calif was both emperor and religious leader to an Islamic realm stretching from northwest India across southwest Asia, on through north Africa, and into Spain.

Bagdad, founded in A.D. 762, was the capital of this empire. Its political importance and its convenient geographical location on the Tigris River made it a prime commercial and trading center. Ships docked there from eastern Africa, India, and China, exchanging goods with caravans trading west to the Mediterranean. The city also benefited from the amazingly rich soil of the Tigris-Euphrates river valley and the thick oak forests of the nearby Zagros Mountains. With its many assets, Bagdad became the richest city in the world.

At the same time, the city became a leading intellectual and cultural center. Encouraged by the califs, great minds and talents emigrated there, representing many nations, religions, disciplines, and traditions. Science, medicine, and literature rose to heights not equaled in Europe for many centuries. When the craft of papermaking arrived from China, handwritten books proliferated, and in one Bagdad bazaar district alone there were a hundred bookshops!

Sadly, the golden age of Bagdad lasted only about a century from its founding. As the Islamic empire fell apart, the city too was torn—by civil strife, marauders, corruption, rebellion, and finally invasion. In the 1800s, Bagdad regained a portion of its prosperity, and in the 1900s became the capital of oil-rich Iraq—but has once more seen its riches drained and destroyed by armed struggle.

Calif is pronounced "KAY-lif." *Vizier,* pronounced "Viz-ZEER," is a prime minister. *Allah,* pronounced "AH-LAH," is the Arabic word for "God."